POTATO CHIP BOOKS

SO GOOD YOU CAN'T STOP READING THEM!

Cat Snacks

Written by Marilyn Pitt & Jane Hileman

Illustrated by John Bianchi

I like this.

This is for me.

I like this.

I like that.

I want this.

I want that.

I love this.

And I love that.

I have to get that.

Can I have this?